For Ainsley, who taught me to see

With thanks to Sara Heise Graybeal, Karen Li,
Wendi Lulu Gu, Dazzle Ng, Molly Rookwood,
Sara Burgess and Carl Cunningham.
In memory of Russ Porter.

Published in 2024 by
Groundwood Books / House of Anansi Press
groundwoodbooks.com

We gratefully acknowledge for their financial support of our publishing program the Canada Council for the Arts, the Ontario Arts Council and the Government of Canada.

 Canada Council   Conseil des Arts
for the Arts   du Canada

 ONTARIO ARTS COUNCIL
CONSEIL DES ARTS DE L'ONTARIO
an Ontario government agency
un organisme du gouvernement de l'Ontario

With the participation of the Government of Canada
Avec la participation du gouvernement du Canada | Canadä

Library and Archives Canada Cataloguing in Publication
Title: All that grows / words and pictures by Jack Wong.
Names: Wong, Jack, author, illustrator.
Identifiers: Canadiana (print) 20230462553 | Canadiana (ebook) 2023046257X | ISBN 9781773068121 (hardcover) | ISBN 9781773068138 (EPUB) | ISBN 9781773068145 (Kindle)
Subjects: LCGFT: Picture books. | LCGFT: Fiction.
Classification: LCC PS8645.O459 A79 2024 | DDC jC813/.6—dc23

The illustrations for this book were created with pastels.
Design by Michael Solomon
Printed and bound in China

 MIX
Paper | Supporting responsible forestry
FSC® C144853
FSC
www.fsc.org

All That Grows

WORDS AND PICTURES BY

JACK WONG

GROUNDWOOD BOOKS
HOUSE OF ANANSI PRESS
TORONTO / BERKELEY

Magnolias smell like lemon cake.

At least, that's what my sister says. They just smell like flowers to me.

On our neighborhood walks, she tells me lots of things.

"This quince tree gets
the most beautiful red in full
bloom," she says. "But the
fruit's only sweet enough
to eat when it grows in
warmer places."

When daffodils start popping up everywhere, even in muddy ditches, my sister tells me they're the flower of Mother's Day. We pick a bouquet to give to Mom — after rinsing off the dirt, of course.

Overnight, the trees go
from bare to bursting with
leaves, turning the streets
into enormous green caverns.
   But in my sister's garden,
the weeds are growing faster
than her vegetable seedlings
under all that shade.

"Want to help?" she asks.

We pick out crabgrass and clover, while leaving the sprouts of radishes and beets. It's hard work not to mistake one for the other, and more weeds come up every day.

My sister gives up on an especially bad patch, but I keep watering it to see what grows.

I wonder why only some plants are called vegetables when my sister says you can eat the greens of a wild dandelion with spaghetti and fry its roots like hash browns.

"They get bitter after flowering, so you have to recognize the leaves to harvest them early."

But then there would be no
yellow dandelion fields, and no
dandelion seeds to blow.

I wonder why some plants are called
flowers, and others are called weeds.

And how some can be both, like goutweed,
which people used to call ground elder and
planted in flower beds on purpose.

Or why we have to keep pulling up the new saplings that come from our neighbor's Norway maples.

My sister says they grow faster than thistle, but I think I'd like to have a little forest — maybe even a treehouse!

Mom brings home a bundle of fiddleheads,
fresh from the market.

   They look a bit like curled-up caterpillars …
which my sister thinks is a good way to
describe them.

   "They're actually the tender leaves
of ferns before they stretch out,"
she says between mouthfuls.

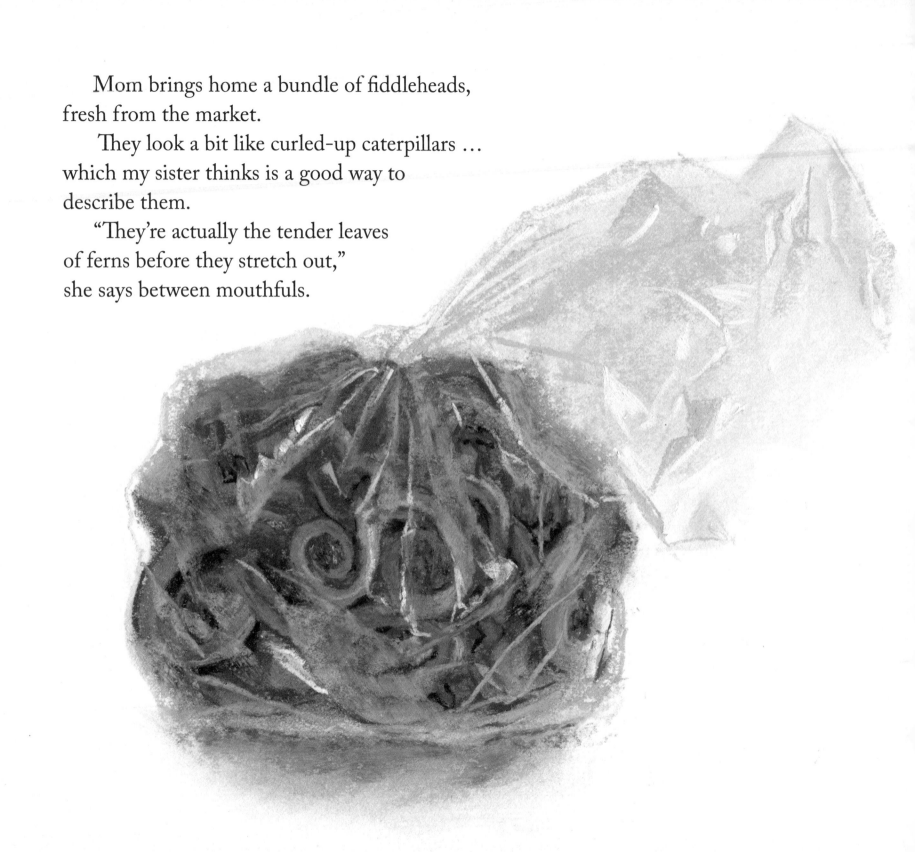

I have to admit, they're good — soft and buttery!
"One more thing —"

"— you can only eat them cooked.

They'll make you sick for days
if you have them raw."

All of these things swirl in my
head, along with one big question.
How does my sister know?

I still can't name the
tree outside my window.
    Beyond the leaves, the
Big Dipper hangs high
in the sky, and I wonder
how we know which
stars belong to which
constellations …

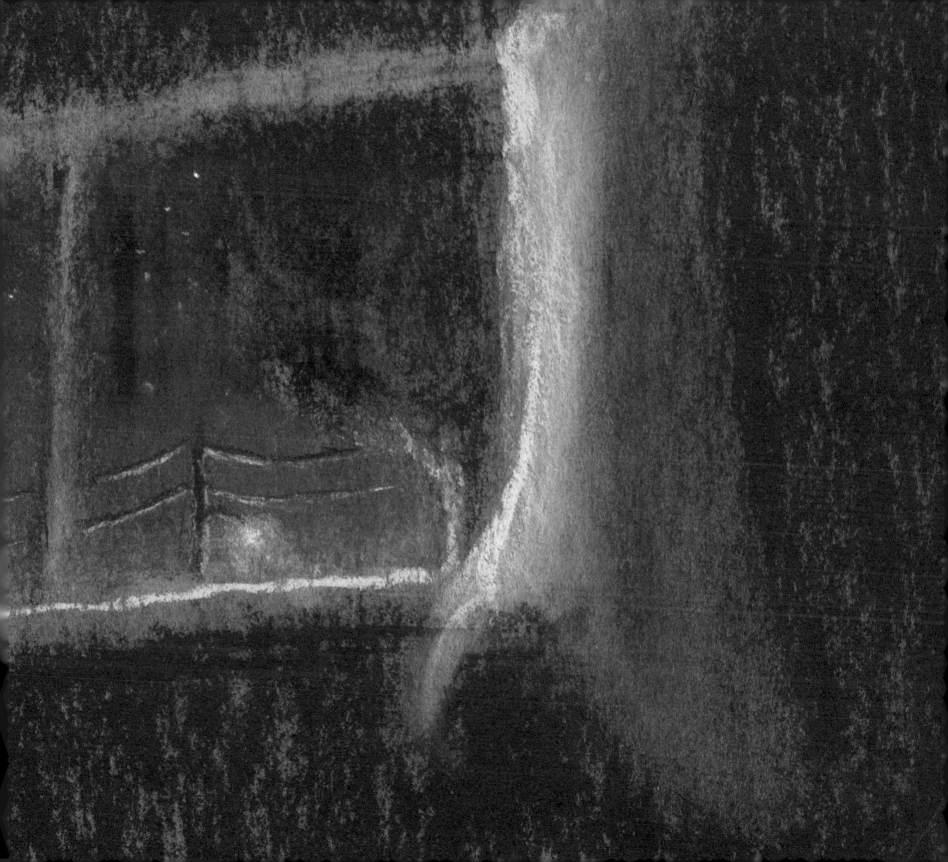

In the weedy patch, delicate white flowers open from little buds. They're something other than the radishes and beets we planted, or the crabgrass and clover we pulled out by the roots. I ask my sister what they are.

She shrugs. "Never seen those before."

Then she examines them again. "Maybe we can look them up in one of my books."

Maybe later.

Right now, I ask her to
help fetch more water for
my garden.